This Ladybird Book belongs to:

BAMFORTH

This Ladybird retelling
by
Audrey Daly

Ladybird books are widely available, but in case of
difficulty may be ordered by post or telephone from:

Ladybird Books – Cash Sales Department
Littlegate Road Paignton Devon TQ3 3BE
Telephone 0803 554761

A catalogue record for this book is available
from the British Library

Published by Ladybird Books Ltd Loughborough Leicestershire UK
Ladybird Books Inc Auburn Maine 04210 USA

FAVOURITE TALES

The Gingerbread Man

illustrated
by
PETER STEVENSON

based on a traditional folk tale

Once upon a time, a little old woman and a little old man lived by themselves in a little old house by the side of a road.

One day, the little old woman decided to make a special treat. "I will make a gingerbread man," she said.

So the little old woman made a gingerbread man and put him in the oven to bake. But before long, she heard a tiny voice calling, "Let me out! Let me out!"

The little old woman went to the oven to listen. Then she opened the oven door.

The gingerbread man jumped right out! He skipped across the kitchen and ran straight outside.

The little gingerbread man was on his way down the road before the little old woman and the little old man were out of the house. They couldn't run nearly as fast as he could.

"Stop! We want to eat you. Stop, little gingerbread man!" they cried, quite out of breath.

But the gingerbread man just sang,

"Run, run, as fast as you can,
You can't catch me,
I'm the gingerbread man!"

Soon the gingerbread man met a cow. "Stop, little man!" mooed the cow. "You look very good to eat!"

But the gingerbread man just ran faster. And he sang,

> *"Run, run, as fast as you can,*
> *You can't catch me,*
> *I'm the gingerbread man!"*

The cow ran and ran, but she could not catch the little gingerbread man.

Farther down the road, the gingerbread man met a horse. "Stop, little man!" said the horse. "You look *very* good to eat, and I'm hungry!"

But the gingerbread man just ran faster.

The horse galloped and galloped as fast as he could, but he wasn't fast enough to catch the gingerbread man.

"I have run away from a little old woman, a little old man, and a cow," cried the gingerbread man. And he sang as he ran,

"Run, run, as fast as you can,
You can't catch me,
I'm the gingerbread man!"

The little gingerbread man ran on
and on, going faster and faster.
He was very proud of his running,
and quite pleased with himself.

At last he met a sly old fox. "Stop!
Stop, little man," said the fox,
grinning and licking his lips. "I
want to talk to you."

But the gingerbread man didn't
stop to listen. He just sang,

"Run, run, as fast as you can,
You can't catch me,
I'm the gingerbread man!"

The cunning old fox could run
very fast indeed, and he ran after
the gingerbread man. He followed
him all the way down the path
through the forest.

Before too long they came to a river. The gingerbread man didn't know what to do.

The cunning old fox wasn't far away. "I'll help you," he said, smiling to himself. "If you jump onto my tail, I will take you across. You will be quite safe and dry."

So the little gingerbread man jumped onto the fox's tail and the fox began to swim across the river.

Very soon the fox said, "You are too heavy for my tail. Jump onto my back."

The little gingerbread man
jumped onto the fox's back.

Very soon the fox said, "Little
gingerbread man, you are too
heavy for my back. Why don't you
jump onto my nose?"

And the little gingerbread man
jumped onto the fox's nose.

Finally they reached the other
side of the river. The fox threw
back his head and tossed the
gingerbread man
high in the air.

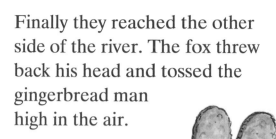

Then *down* fell the
gingerbread man,
and *snap!* went
the old fox.

And that was
the end of the little
gingerbread man.